The
LITTLE LAME PRINCE
✳ ROSEMARY ✳ WELLS ✳

Based on a story by Dinah Maria Mulock Craik

Dial Books for Young Readers *New York*

Published by Dial Books for Young Readers
A Division of Penguin Books USA Inc.
375 Hudson Street
New York, New York 10014

Printed in Hong Kong by
South China Printing Company (1988) Limited
Design by Jane Byers Bierhorst
E
First Edition

Library of Congress Cataloging in Publication Data

Wells, Rosemary.
The little lame prince / by Rosemary Wells.
p. cm.
"Based on a story by Dinah Maria Mulock Craik."
Summary: A young crippled prince must reclaim his
kingdom from his evil uncle, with the help of
a magic cape from his godmother.
ISBN 0-8037-0788-6. ISBN 0-8037-0789-4 (lib. bdg.)
[1. Fairy tales. 2. Physically handicapped—Fiction.]
I. Craik, Dinah Maria Mulock, 1826–1887. Little lame prince. II. Title.
PZ8.W455Li 1990 89-23482 [E]—dc20 CIP AC

The artwork for each picture
is a watercolor painting on paper.

✳

The Little Lame Prince
is inspired by the novel of the same name by the
English author Dinah Maria Mulock Craik. First
published in 1874, *The Little Lame Prince* did not
go out of print for over one hundred years, appearing in
at least seventy separate editions and illustrated
by numerous artists in the United States alone.

Once upon a time, in the land of El Cordoba, a Prince was born. His mother, the Queen, and his father, the King, called him Francisco and doted on him endlessly. Francisco was a healthy baby with a beautiful complexion and intelligent eyes the color of the sky.

Sadly, the Queen was often ill and so the King spent many hours by her bedside rocking Francisco and singing to him while the Queen played for him on her little harp.

On Prince Francisco's first birthday El Cordoba went wild with celebration. Vats of the best cider were opened. Ten kinds of fruit juice were squeezed. Three tons of spiced kumquats were fried up and zucchini muffins were baked for everyone in the kingdom.

But that day the Queen was so ill she could not attend the party. She gave Francisco to a chambermaid to carry. She chose the prettiest one.

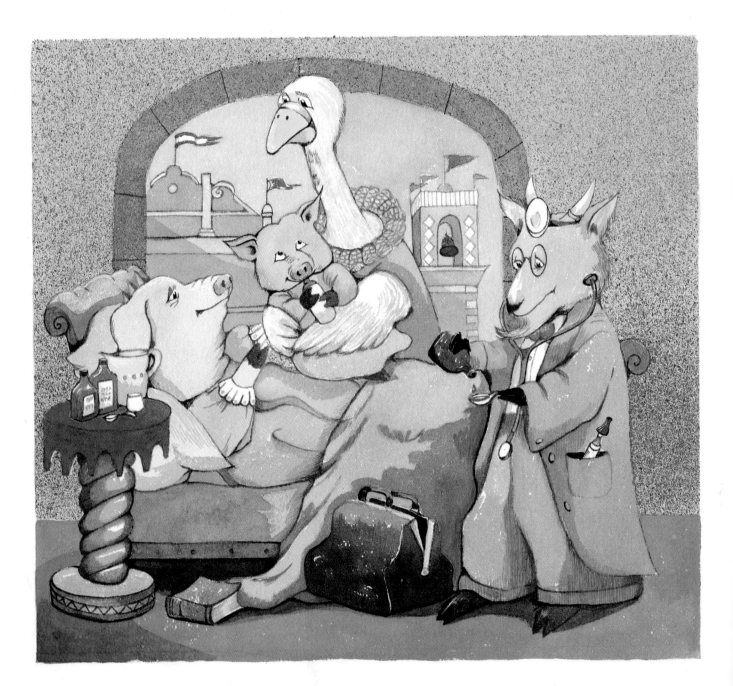

That was a mistake. Just before the start of the Grand March the pretty chambermaid decided to fix her eyelashes. She held Francisco carelessly. Francisco gave a little lurch and fell heavily on the marble floor.

To the chambermaid's horror he did not cry but turned the color of dead leaves instead.

"Pick him up, you dumb cluck!" rasped a cracked voice from inside an urn. A spry little woman appeared.

"Who do you think you are? You little snip!" huffed the chambermaid.

"I am the Prince's godmother, that's who!" cackled the old woman. "And I am going to watch you like a hawk all day long, my dear!" Then, with a sound exactly like the popping of corn, the old woman vanished.

The birthday continued without a hitch. As far as the guilty chambermaid could tell, the little Prince's color began to seep into his face, but he didn't wiggle in her arms.

No one noticed anything until four o'clock that afternoon when the bell in the tower began tolling. Upstairs in the palace the Queen had died in her sleep.

In the weeks that followed, the King fell into a deep and shadowy gloom. He cried without stopping, losing thirty pounds. He would not eat or do any work. Soon he would not even get up and get dressed.

The King allowed his brother, Osvaldo, to take over some of his duties. This was a terrible mistake. After a year Osvaldo was running everything.

In the meantime Prince Francisco had been nearly forgotten.
He grew happily in the care of a nice nurse from one of the local
farms. He was perfectly healthy except that he could not move
his legs. One of the gardeners made him a little wheelchair
out of apple wood.

At the end of another two years the King had shriveled
to sixty pounds and could barely lift a glass of water to his lips.
No doctor could help him. Osvaldo, his porky wife, Isabella, and
their seven wild and whiney sons moved into the royal palace.

El Cordoba was a very unhappy country under Osvaldo's rule. The farmers were paid nothing for their crops. The shopkeepers had to give their best goods to Osvaldo's palace guards. But worst of all Osvaldo closed the shelters for the poor and homeless and cut off supplies of milk for the orphans. Soldiers were everywhere wearing expensive uniforms. The soldiers shoved people around.

Within a few weeks the King was dead.

Now only a three-year-old Prince, one who couldn't even walk, stood between Osvaldo and the throne of El Cordoba. One night after an enormous dinner Osvaldo chuckled and murmured, "Tonight I will push Francisco out of a window and he will drop into the palace moat."

At that moment the sound of popping corn interrupted his giggling.

Francisco's godmother emerged from the humidor. "You evil lump of lard!" she declared. "If you harm a hair on Francisco's head, I will see to it a vat of boiling grease falls on you!"

Osvaldo believed in magic and so was terrified of the little godmother. He came up with a new plan to get rid of Francisco without harming him.

The next night he summoned a poor woman from jail who had been condemned to death for stealing apples. Her name was Carmen.

"Miserable woman!" growled Osvaldo. "I am sending you to Tierra Dolorosa, the coldest and most remote place on earth. There you will live in a tower and care for my nephew, Francisco. If you ever tell him he is Prince of El Cordoba, you will be sentenced to death again!"

Carmen and Prince Francisco were piled into a single railway coach. It was loaded with supplies and driven by an engineer who could only speak an Eskimo language that no one could understand. They left for Tierra Dolorosa at midnight.

The tower in Tierra Dolorosa stood at the end of the world. Nothing but crabgrass grew in the sandy earth as far as the eye

could see, and a damp, rheumatic wind blew every day, twelve
months a year.

Every now and then the engineer would come back with fresh
supplies, but he could not understand a word Carmen said.
With no one to talk to, Carmen taught Francisco how to sing,
recite poetry, and speak like a grown-up.

Francisco grew and learned to read. He grew more and
learned to count. Always he tried to walk like Carmen. "No,
Francisco," Carmen told him. "You must sit in your wheelchair.
Your legs are useless."

Still Francisco crawled up and down the stairs and all over
the tower. He read every book the engineer brought. He read
the labels on every jar in the kitchen, and he read the letters that
Carmen's sister, Rosa, sent telling of a troubled El Cordoba
under Osvaldo's cruel reign.

From the books Francisco learned that he was not like other
children who could run and skip and jump.

One dreary day when Francisco was eleven years old and the raindrops coursed down the windowpane like tears, Francisco put down the book he'd read ten times and grumbled, "I want to walk! I want to play football like other boys!"

Suddenly he heard the strange snap of popping corn. Out of an unused flower pot on the balcony, a little old lady appeared. "Hello!" she said.

"Hello," said Francisco. "Who are you?"

"I am your godmother," said the lady.

"You must be magic," said Francisco.

"I am," she answered, "but with limited powers. Look!" and she unrolled her cape on the floor. It appeared to be a large green lily pad. "Lots of boys and girls can run," she said, "but very few can fly. Get on it and tell it to go!"

Francisco did as he was told. He sat in the middle of the cape and told it, "Up! Up!" expecting nothing. Zoom! the cape lifted him three feet off the floor.

"If you need me, call me," said his godmother and she vanished with the popcorn sound.

Francisco did nothing but experiment with his cape from that moment on. Fortunately for him the rainy weather gave Carmen a series of migraine headaches, and he had plenty of undisturbed time. At last he got the cape to go out the window.

Soon Francisco was able to travel great distances. He sped out of Tierra Dolorosa and swooped over the Sangria Mountains. He circled the outlying villages of his homeland, but he never went near the capital of El Cordoba. Francisco was frightened by what Carmen read to him about Osvaldo in her sister's letters.

Francisco did not want Carmen to know about his cape, but since she spent so much time in bed these days he was free to come and go as he pleased.

One night, after a beautiful flight down the Corona D'Oro River valley, Francisco arrived back in time for supper, as he usually did. He noticed the supply coach was just pulling away.

Francisco peeked in the kitchen window. Carmen was reading one of her sister's letters. Tears filled her eyes and her limbs shook as she read it.

Over supper Carmen read the letter aloud. "Osvaldo is breaking the hearts of our noble El Cordobans," she explained to Francisco. "At this very moment farms are burning and shops are being looted by Osvaldo's soldiers. The country is in revolution! My poor sister is so hungry and frightened," Carmen sobbed.

"What can we do?" asked Francisco.

Carmen took Francisco's arm and told him the secret she had kept for so many years. "You . . . you are the rightful King of El Cordoba, Francisco," she whispered. "Osvaldo is your uncle!"

"I?" asked Francisco in disbelief.

"Yes," said Carmen. "It is a tragedy you are only a crippled boy and can do nothing."

That night Francisco flounced sleeplessly in his bed. "I am the King of El Cordoba," he said, "but I can't walk. People will laugh at me, a little lame boy in a wheelchair. What can I do?"

As if to answer him, the noise of popping corn crackled through the air. Francisco's godmother emerged from a wardrobe and stood patiently at the foot of his bed.

"Francisco," she said, "you are a king. It is time to act like one. Get a good night's sleep. Eat a big breakfast in the morning, and go and help your people in their hour of need!"

Francisco was up before the few birds of Tierra Dolorosa awoke. Hurriedly he told Carmen the secret of his cape. She made him a breakfast of blueberry muffins, melon, cocoa, strawberries and cream, a Swiss cheese omelet, and banana supreme. Then she kissed him good-bye.

He flew all day into the heart of El Cordoba. By midnight
Francisco reached the capital.

Only one light glowed at the palace. In the state dining room
Osvaldo and Isabella had finished off a gargantuan dinner.

From where he hovered in the dark, Francisco could see
Osvaldo spoon a chocolate cream puff with caramel sauce
into his mouth. He washed it down with a slug of brandy and
lit a cigar.

Suddenly Isabella turned and spotted Francisco. "Mother of
all the saints!" she shrieked. "Osvaldo, call the guards!"

Osvaldo wiped his mouth on his sleeve and staggered to
the window. "Who in the name of Lucifer are you?" he trumpeted.

"I am your nephew, Francisco," Francisco answered politely.

"I must be drunk," muttered Osvaldo and he reached for
the coffee.

After downing two or three cups he peered out the window
at Francisco again. *"Sacre Escombro!"* he cried. "I recognize his
face!"

At that moment a tremor shuddered through Osvaldo's body. The cigars, the brandy, the coffee, and the huge, greasy meals that Osvaldo had consumed over the years had taken their toll. Congealing with the shame and evil in his soul, the combination dropped Osvaldo dead at Isabella's feet. Isabella wept.

"I'm sorry. I didn't mean to kill him," said Francisco, gliding
into the room.

"Young man, these are tears of joy!" sobbed Isabella.
"Osvaldo was a cruel husband. He bought me expensive gifts,
but he had the heart of a toad. Now I can take my precious boys
back to my mother in Madrid." She sniffed into her hanky. "You
poor dear, you must be starving," she said. "Have some salmon
stuffed with wild mushrooms and caviar."

"No, thank you," said Francisco. "I will not eat until the
people of El Cordoba are fed."

The next morning Francisco opened the jails and let
everyone innocent go free. He declared a feast day and, using
Osvaldo's private kitchens, he ordered up enough mango pasta,
coconut surprise, banana supreme, and fried kumquats for
the whole kingdom.

Late that night, when the feast was over and all the hungry mouths fed, Francisco rested at last. As he fell asleep in his wheelchair he sighed and said, "I hope I will be a good king. I hope no one will laugh at my useless legs."

From a hand-painted bowl full of fruit came the sudden sound of corn popping. It was Francisco's godmother. "You will be the best-loved king in the history of El Cordoba," she said. "No one cares about your legs when your head is wise and your heart is kind."

Ever after Francisco ruled his kingdom from a wheelchair. From time to time Carmen still pushed him around the palace. Soon the chair was festooned with flowers, coins, and gifts from his grateful citizens.

But some nights, when the moon was full and the world was asleep, Francisco went flying secretly on his magic cape, over the mountains and valleys, to listen to faraway music and to watch distant villages glistening in the dark.